DISNEP
Winnie the Pooh
Better Than Honey?

DISNEP PRESS

Good morning, Winnie the Pooh thought to himself with a yawn. What shall I do today?

Pooh thought about his question as he climbed out of bed. By the time he'd finished doing his stoutness exercises, he'd come up with an answer.

"I believe it would be a fine day for some honey," he said.

Feeling pleased with his decision, Pooh went to his cupboard. There were several honeypots on the shelves. But there was no honey inside any of them.

"Oh, bother," Pooh said. "I forgot that I ate all of my honey yesterday. Perhaps I will visit Rabbit."

"Good morning, Rabbit," Pooh said politely. "Have you had breakfast yet?"

Rabbit looked suspicious. "Yes," he said. "Haven't you?"

"Why, no. I haven't. Thank you for inviting me," Pooh said.

Soon, Pooh was enjoying a smackerel of honey. "I never tasted such delicious honey," he said in a sticky voice.

"I never knew someone so obsessed with honey." Rabbit sounded a bit cross. "Don't you ever do anything but eat honey, Pooh Bear?"

Pooh stopped eating. "I suppose I must do other things sometimes, mustn't I?" Pooh said. "The trouble is, I can't quite think of what those things might be just now.

"What are you going to do today, Rabbit?" Pooh continued. "Perhaps I could do the same thing."

"I'm going to work in my garden," Rabbit answered.

Pooh didn't know much about gardening. But he agreed to give it a try. First he helped Rabbit pick some carrots.

Then they watered the peas and mulched the tomatoes.

Pooh enjoyed all of it. It wasn't the same as eating honey. But it was fun to try something different.

"That's enough gardening, Pooh," Rabbit said after a while.
"Why don't you go find something else to do?"

"Like eating honey?" Pooh said hopefully. "Is there any more?"

"No," Rabbit replied. "You'll have to think of something else."

Pooh wandered off, thinking as hard as he could. Then he noticed that he was near Owl's house.

Owl is the wisest friend I have, Pooh said to himself. Perhaps he'll be able to help me figure out what to do now.

Owl listened to Pooh's dilemma. "This puts me in mind of my great-aunt Phyllis," he said. "She loved trying new things. Knitting, baking, checkers, camel racing, fly-tying . . ."

Owl went on and on and on. Finally he suggested that Pooh try writing his memoirs.

Pooh was just beginning to write when Eeyore came by.

"What are you doing, Eeyore?" Pooh asked.

Eeyore sighed. "Going to the thistle patch for lunch."

"May I join you, Eeyore?" Pooh asked. "Thistles for lunch sounds like a delicious new thing to try."

"Well?" Eeyore asked Pooh. "How do you like the thistles?"

"They're, er, different," Pooh said politely, picking a prickly bit of thistle out of his tongue. "They'd probably be even tastier with a smackerel of honey."

Just then, Tigger bounced into view. "Hoo-hoo-hoo!" he cried when he saw Pooh. "What's new, Buddy Bear?"

"A lot," Pooh said. "I'm trying interesting new things today."

"You are?" Tigger said. "Then how's about you try some bouncing? It's the *abso-tively* most *inneresting* thing there is!"

"It is?" Pooh said. "Then I suppose I should try it."

Pooh and Tigger bounced together for a while.

"Whaddaya think, Buddy Bear?" Tigger said.

"It's very interesting," Pooh replied breathlessly, "but rather tiring. And it does make one a bit hungry."

They bounced toward Piglet's house. "Watch this!"
Tigger told Pooh. "Hello, Piglet!"

He bounced Piglet right off his feet. "H-hello, Tigger,"
Piglet said. "Hello, Pooh. What are you two doing?"

"We're bouncing," Pooh said. "I'm trying new things today,
Piglet. Can you think of anything I should try?"

"You could help me collect haycorns," Piglet suggested.

As Pooh picked the haycorns, he popped one into his mouth. It wasn't quite as delicious as honey. But it *was* tasty. Pooh ate another one.

The two friends kept collecting haycorns. Strangely, though, Pooh's basket never got much heavier. When there were no more haycorns to collect, Piglet invited Pooh to lunch. But Pooh wasn't hungry.

Pooh went in search of
something else to do. He soon
came upon little Roo playing
in the Sandy Pit.

"Hello, Pooh," Roo said. "Want to build sand sculptures
with me?"

"This is almost as much fun as eating honey!" Pooh said.

Pooh and Piglet played together in the sand until Kanga appeared. "Bath time, Roo," she said.

"Aw, do I have to, Mama?" Roo asked.

"Bath time sounds interesting," Pooh said. "Can I try it, too?"

Kanga sized him up uncertainly. "I'm not sure you *and* the water will both fit in the tub, Pooh," she said. "But I'm sure we can find *something* for you to do."

It turned out that Kanga knew about lots of
interesting new things Pooh could try,

such as sweeping the stoop,

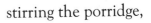

stirring the porridge,

carrying in some apples for supper,

and much more.

Pooh was hanging the laundry out to dry when Christopher Robin appeared. "Hello, Pooh Bear," the boy said. "What have you been up to today?"

"Oh, all sorts of things." Pooh told Christopher Robin about his day. "Some things I tried made me more hungry, and some made me less hungry." Pooh sighed. "But I'm afraid all of them made me think about honey."